Contents

To my children
and in memory of
T. Crofton Croker
who wrote so well
about the Little People

The Little People of Ireland

Up the airy mountain
Down the rushy glen,
We daren't go a-hunting
For fear of little men:
Wee folk, good folk,
Trooping all together;
Green jacket, red cap
And white owl's feather.

Some older people may have learnt and enjoyed this poem by William Allingham in their primary school days, but with the technology and urbanization of our modern world, fairies nowadays are almost forgotten. In Ireland, it is said that they may still be seen occasionally, wearing the red cap and green jacket. However, do not use the name 'fairies' while you are in that country. You might find that the gate to the field where you are picnicking has mysteriously disappeared just when you are about to leave, or slip on a patch of mud on a perfectly dry riverbank while fishing and land in the water, amid shrieks of mocking laughter, although nobody is nearby.

Fairies in Ireland prefer to be known as the 'Little People', the 'Gentry' or the 'Good People'. The adjective 'good' is perhaps a trifle elastic, since the Gentry are often very far from good and get a lot of amusement from playing tricks on unsuspecting humans.

In Ireland, the older generation of country folk used to be 'well able for them' as they say, and would never dream of describing fairies in any other terms. In the same way, to this day, they will not admire a new baby without adding the words 'God bless her (or him)' for fear that they might ill-wish the child and a Changeling (fairy baby) be put in its place. The formula also applies to a particularly fine calf or foal, and I have heard it used by a delighted, Guinness-breathing gentleman about a fine horse at the local point-to-point.

The Little People of Ireland are roughly divided into three kinds: those who live together, solitary fairies and fairy animals.

'What, in the name of fortune am I supposed to do about that!' groaned Jack.

The fact that he believed her showed that he had not, in fact, forgotten all the tales his grandmother told him.

'Move the kitchen,' said his mother-in-law.

'But I only just built it,' wailed Jack.

''Tis the only way to fix it,' she said firmly. 'I'll send Mikey to give a hand.'

News got around, as news does in the country. Nobody actually says anything, but it permeates the area through the odd word or smile from the shop to the pub and in next to no time it has arrived at the most remote of the hill farms.

The couple who had decided to take the bungalow for the winter while their own house was being repaired, pulled out of the deal with an excuse so lame that it was almost an insult. It seemed nobody wanted to take the Ryan's fine new place. The Tourist Board had no further families for him that summer and though they tried private advertising, it cost a lot and brought in nothing.

In the end, Jack, with fury, cursing, the help of his two sons and his brother-in-law Mikey, along with Mikey's invaluable cement mixer, knocked down the offending kitchen and built it up again behind the living room where, truth to tell, it was much more convenient.

From that day, there was no further trouble; his business thrived, his stock were the finest in the area and his mother-in-law, being a wise lady did not say, 'I told you so'.

The only instance of a house remaining untroubled although built across a fairy way occurred a long time ago.

In a certain district in the West, there was a small cottage. Strange things happened there. When the shepherd who occupied it woke in the morning, he would find his stores ransacked, trails of flour and oatmeal across the floor from the front door to the back door which stood opposite it, across the kitchen. He put it down to rats and brought in the dogs. They made the confusion worse by scrabbling among the sacks

The Sidhe

The *Sidhe* (pronounced shee) are the subject of many stories. Their dwelling places are the large green mounds called raths, found all over the country. These often have a thorn tree or two growing on them. A superstitious passer-by will tear a strip from their clothing to tie on the tree or hang a safety pin or other bright object from a twig to bring them luck.

Each rath has its own king and there is one High King who rules over them all. He lives in the great hill of Tara and every year in autumn, kings of the raths and their retinues come to renew their pledge of loyalty to him. You will not see them because they travel like a cloud of autumn leaves, bronze, scarlet and yellow, blown across the countryside.

At night, it is said that a door opens in the side of the rath and the Little People stream out, riding milk-white horses with silver trappings, laughing and singing, with white wolfhounds running before and minstrels playing wonderful music walking behind them. They have pale, proud, strangely beautiful faces, long golden hair and always dress in shining green and silver. Some folk say they are the last of the Tuatha Dé Danaan who once ruled Ireland and were driven underground by the Celts.

The Sidhe certainly love luxury, feasting, dancing and music. They hate meanness and stinginess. If you are lucky enough to receive a fairy gift, it will be magnificent, but be careful if you wish to give them a present. It must be something small and insignificant, a brown egg in a plaited rush basket, or a little silver coin, otherwise they will take umbrage and then you are in trouble!

There was once a farmer's wife living in a comfortable hill farmhouse not too far from a rath. One evening, as she and the young servant girl were preparing the tea, there came a knock on the door. The girl went to open it and there on the step stood a little rath man(the name they used for the Gentry in those parts).

'Good evening,' he said politely. 'We were wondering, could your mistress ever give us the loan of a saucepan? There's a wedding below in the hill and all the pots are in use.'

'Will I give him one?' whispered the girl.

'Indeed you will,' answered the farmer's wife.

The girl went towards the shelf where the pans were stored, but the farmer's wife, who always had an eye on the main chance, whispered, 'Not any of those. Get the one with the hole in it from the press, the one I have laid aside for the travelling people to fix when they come. The hill men will mend it better than ever they could, and save me sixpence at the same time!'

Sure enough, the saucepan came back the next day, neatly mended and she was delighted by her cleverness. At teatime that evening the maidservant filled it with milk to warm up for the children, but the moment she set it on the fire, the milk rose up and boiled over into the flames, the pan scorched and the whole kitchen was filled with smoke and the horrible smell of burnt milk. The farmer's wife scolded the servant girl for being wasteful.

'A quart of good milk spoiled!' she exclaimed crossly and as she did so, a little, high-pitched, grumbling voice came from the chimney.

'That's tuppence!' it said.

The farmer's wife looked round to see who had spoken but nobody was there so she thought she had imagined it, and flounced out into the yard to pour the burnt milk into the pigs' trough but even they would not drink it.

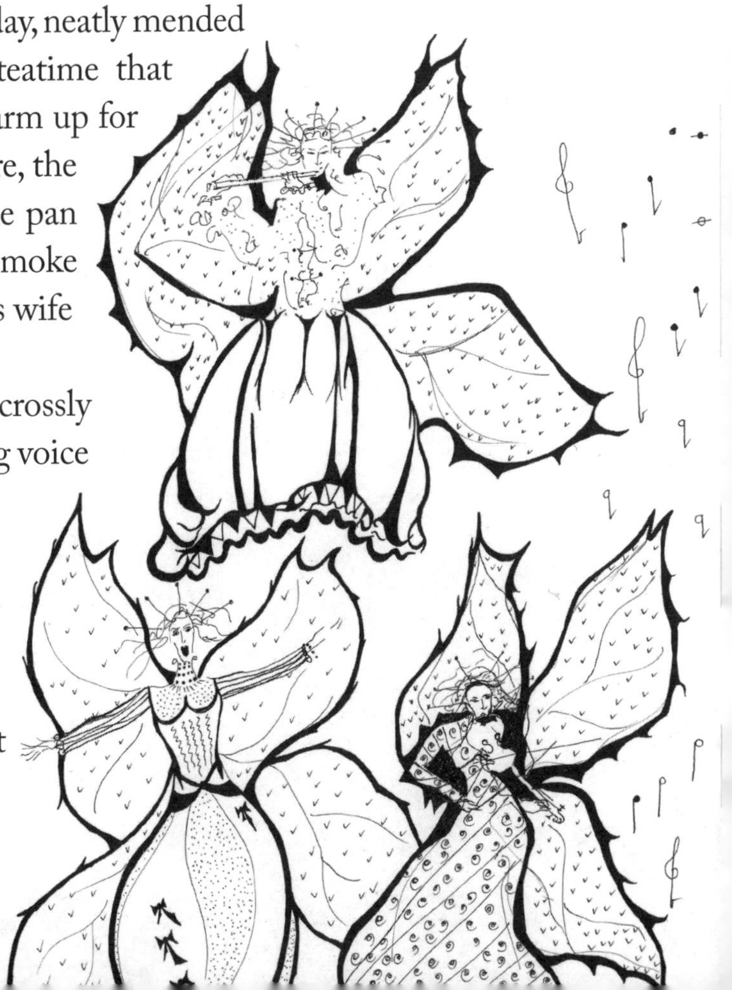

The farmer's wife said that *she* would show the girl how to heat the milk properly *this* time, but the same thing happened and the servant had a good laugh to herself as she scoured the pan at the sink.

Meanwhile from the chimney, the same little voice exclaimed crossly, 'An' that's fourpence!'

Mortified at the waste, the farmer's wife tried again and again the milk burned.

'Ochone, ochone! I'm housekeeping the best part of me life and never before did I spoil six quarts of milk!' she cried, throwing herself down on the settle and bursting into tears.

The grumpy voice came from the chimney again, 'An' that's *sixpence*!'

The little rath man came scrambling down the chimney laughing fit to burst.

'So you didn't save the money for the travelling people after all!' he shouted, as he whisked out of the door leaving them speechless.

The saucepan was put away at the back of the press and never used until one day the wife's mother, who was visiting, fetched it out not knowing the story. When she heard what had happened, she gave her daughter a good scolding for being so mean, and oddly enough, the pan never again burned anything.

It never pays to be stingy with the Sidhe, for you won't get the better of them!

Special feast days for the Sidhe are the ancient Beltaine, which is the first of May, Midsummer and Samhain or Hallowe'en.

On May Eve, they can sometimes be seen dancing in the fields. Maeve O'Grady saw them one night, footing it on the dewy grass of the long field by the river. She was standing in the deep shadows beneath the hazel trees, waiting for her lover. The music drew her unwillingly towards the cheerful throng and before she knew where she was, she was dancing away with small, graceful men, round dumpy Cluricauns and all manner of strange beings.

She returned home as dawn was just colouring the sky in the East, with her dancing shoes quite worn out, to find a month had passed. Her family were frantic, fearing she had been drowned or abducted. Her lover had gone off with another girl, yet she steadfastly continued to believe that she had only been absent for one night.

At Midsummer, the Sidhe go to war with clans from other raths for the choicest ears of corn from the farmer's fields for their storerooms, the best butter and anything else they fancy. You cannot see the little warriors with their silver helmets and breastplates, but if you are out of doors at harvest time, watch for a small whirlwind moving across the stackyard, or over the stubble where the sheaves are being loaded, picking up straws and blowing dust into the workers' eyes. Country people call these miniature tornados 'sheegwees', or fairy winds, and you can be sure there is a battle going on in the midst of it. If you are wise, you will tip your hat when you see such winds, or knuckle your forehead and say 'Good morning, good sirs,' so that they do not feel slighted. After all, who wants a mouthful of dust? They are also said to ride magpies, so you should always greet a single magpie by saluting it and saying 'Good morning, my lord' in case it is carrying a passenger.

In autumn, the Sidhe celebrate as humans used to do, dancing around hilltop fires, though if you mistake the firelight for a human bonfire, and hope to join the fun, you will find nothing but a ring of fairy toadstools when you get there. Like humans, they play tricks at Hallowe'en too and were said to be the originators of 'trick or treat'. Sensible householders put out saucers of cream and perhaps a small cake of curranty soda bread, carefully not marked with the habitual cross on the top, as the Little People will not go near a Christian symbol. This small kindness would avert unexpected winds blowing down the chimney, scattering ashes over the clean hearthstone, and choking those sitting beside it.

Loud knocking on doors in the dark, for all the world as if the Garda were outside might also occur to annoy the householder. This resulted in many a fright and a scramble as an illicit bottle of poteen was shoved into the back of the press or into the flour bin, before the door was answered to reveal – nobody. Though you may be sure there was a lot of laughter floating down the breeze.

Another trick was teasing the farm dogs till they began to bark, forcing people from the warm fireside to light lanterns and investigate the cause of the hullabaloo. Then the Gentry would blow out the lights and laugh heartily as humans stumbled cursing about in the yard in the darkness.

It must have been a sad day for the Sidhe when the electric torch was invented, followed by the Rural Electrification Scheme, which put lights in the yard and byre and did away with a little trick they had of muddying the cobblestones by the doorway, causing some misfortunate milker to slip with a full bucket, the contents of which was delightedly received by the Little People.

The Sidhe dislike the short days and the rain and cold of winter and spend their time in the rath, feasting and merrymaking. On fine frosty, moonlit nights though, they can sometimes be seen setting out on a hunting expedition with their white wolfhounds. They shout in high, shrill, almost inaudible voices, like bats, among the tough heather stems of the hillsides or the silvered brambles and leafless trees in winter woods. Humans who hear the sound of their hunting horns put it down to the sizzling of damp logs on the open fire or a passing car in the distance, but children and certain adults, who have not forgotten their youth, know that it is not and perhaps feel a shade of regret for bygone days.

The Sidhe travel on fairy roads that cover the length and breadth of Ireland and strongly object to any obstruction in their path. There is an interesting story about this.

It was the time when farming was not so profitable. Farmers were looking about for other ways to make money and some decided that it might be a good idea to build a house on their land for holiday letting. Jack Ryan was one of them and with the help of his two sons he erected a pleasant long bungalow with a view across the valley to the distant sea.

There was great excitement in the farmhouse when the first tenants arrived for their summer holiday. They were country people themselves, with a large family of children and found the experience most enjoyable. The parents became friendly with the Ryans and the children had run of the fields and farmyard. Being country bred, they had been brought up to shut gates to keep in the stock. Also, again being country bred, the house was usually left open when they were out in the neighbourhood.

However things were different when the second party of holidaymakers arrived. They came from the Continent but fortunately the parents spoke good English and they settled in quite happily, delighted with the fresh eggs, milk and loaf of soda bread the Ryans had left in their kitchen to 'start them off'.

A few days later, the husband came down to the farm and asked to speak to Jack.

'Have you a second key to the house?' asked the tenant.

'Yes,' replied Jack.

'Well, we would appreciate you didn't use it to get into the house while we are out,' said the man stiffly. 'You did not lock the back door when you left and well—,' he shifted uncomfortably and reddened, 'in our country it is not customary to enter people's houses when they are not there—even landlords respect privacy—.'

'But I was never in the house!' exclaimed Jack, annoyed that he was thought to be lacking in courtesy in a country that was noted for it.

'Perhaps someone else,' suggested the tenant, noting his anger.

Jack asked the rest of the family. Nobody had been in the house. The tenant went away but was back again within two days with the same complaint. Every morning they found the back door open.

Jack changed the lock but the same thing happened. He fitted extra bolts but still the door would not stay shut. The tenants left in a huff, and Jack wondered what on earth was happening. He sat up in the bungalow kitchen with his twelve bore gun for two nights but saw nobody and found the door open in the morning, just as the tenants had said. He cursed himself for nodding off the first night and fortified himself with a flask of strong coffee for the second, but that did not seem to work either and began to wonder if he was going mad.

It was not until his wife's mother came for a visit that the mystery was solved.

'Lord save us, Jack, did ye never listen to the old stories when you were a lad?' chuckled the elderly lady when she heard the tale of woe. 'Sure, you're after building your fine new house across a fairy road! Of course, the door won't stay shut!'

with great enthusiasm but no results, eventually overturning a bag of sugar which stuck to paws and boots with great impartiality. After this mishap was dealt with, there was no trouble until a few weeks later, when the trails appeared again. This time, the shepherd noticed the prints of tiny feet in the flour, crossing and re-crossing the room. He knew what that meant and went to his master. He explained what had happened and begged to be housed elsewhere until shearing was completed. The farmer, who valued his shepherd agreed and his cottage remained empty.

After a while, a rumour that the place was haunted got about and nobody would live there. The master had to arrange other accommodation for his workers and the little house was left to crumble away.

Then one day a poor old woman came to the farmhouse. She had walked all the way from Ennis, she said. Her feet were bound in rags, for her shoes had worn out on the long road and she was starving.

The farmer's wife brought her inside and gave her a meal.

While they sat at the fire over a cup of tea, little by little, her story emerged. Her husband had been killed by a bull at the place where he worked, and although she had a job in the kitchen and dairy there, the owner had turned her out of her cottage to make room for another, younger couple. He had sent her off with her week's wages, refusing to pay what was due to her husband, because he said that the man had been careless moving the bull from his pen and deserved what had had happened to him.

The farmer's wife was horrified at such ill treatment and resolved to do whatever she could for the poor woman. Unfortunately, there was no room at the farm, for she had a large family, but she made a bed on the settle by the fire for her.

When her husband came in, she explained what she had done.

The farmer frowned. 'What in the wide earthly world are we to do with her?' he said. 'We've no place fit for her—Unless—'

His wife was quick-thinking. 'You mean the cottage? The one your Grandda's shepherd used to live in?'

He nodded. 'We'd have to tell her—'

The next day they explained their predicament. The old woman wept with gratitude at their kindness and insisted that, of course, she would be all right in the 'houseen'. Never mind if it was haunted, sure maybe it was only a ghost that did not like men!

The farmer patched up the holes in the roof and walls and she was delighted. They gave her some supplies with the promise of a wage for light work around the farm and she moved in.

A few days later, as evening was drawing in and the sun setting over the bay in a riot of scarlet and yellow, like a swathe of shot silk against the grey sea, a knock came at the front door.

Opening it, the old woman found a tall and beautiful lady standing on the doorstep.

'Good evening to you, ma'am. May I borrow some oats?' she asked politely.

The old woman gave her all she had and the next day at the same time the beautiful lady returned to pay her debt.

Having had the time to think about it, the old woman suspected that the lady might be from the great rath in the valley about a mile away and knowing the ways of the Good People wisely refused to take anything.

'Ye made good use of the oats, I'm sure,' she said, 'and I'm not in the want of them.'

'But you must take something,' said the lady. ''Tisn't our way not to repay a kindness.'

She thought for a moment, and then said, 'If you will keep the back door of this house shut all the time, you can stay there forever and we won't trouble you at all at all.'

She was true to her word and the Good People, for once, must have moved their pathway for the old woman had no bother at all, and lived in the cottage till the end of her days in perfect peace and comfort.

But she never opened the back door.

It is said that the music of the Sidhe would 'call the heart out of ye forever'. Carolan, the harper, was the most famous of all Irish bards. He travelled the country from North to South and was welcome in the halls of the great as he was among the cottages of the poor. One evening he was far out in the hills and took a rest in a comfortable hollow under a thorn tree. He fell asleep, not realizing that he was lying on a rath but he came to no harm, for the Good People loved his airs as much as humans and ever after, the tunes of the Sidhe ran in his head and were found in his music.

Some of the old and beautiful songs, like 'The Pretty Maid Milking Her Cow' are said to be of fairy origin, picked up by the eavesdroppers near the raths, but the Gentry hate to hear their music on mortal lips, so take care where you sing or whistle. You may find yourself tormented with nips and pinches, or a persistent ringing in your ears.

The only person whose singing they tolerated was the hunchback Lusmore. He got his name from the sprig of foxglove (*Lus Mór* in Irish) that he wore in his hat. Though handicapped, he made a living weaving baskets and straw hats for harvesters. He was always merry and ready to help anyone.

One summer evening, returning from selling his wares at the fair in a nearby town, he sat down to rest his tired legs on the low, ivy-covered wall beside an old castle.

Presently he heard the Sidhe singing a cheerful, catchy tune among the ruins.

Lusmore was not afraid of them. He often saw them on moonlit nights when he was walking around the fields to ease the pains in his back which kept him awake. He listened awhile and finding the song monotonous, waited for a pause then added a few lines of his own. Lusmore was blessed with a fine voice and the Good People were delighted. They crowded round and begged him to teach them the new music. Patiently, he sang it over a few times. When they had learned it, they thanked him heartily and one tall fellow, who seemed to be the chief among them, clapped him on the back.

Immediately, his hump fell off and he stood up straight for the first time in his life. Not only that, but he had a whole new suit of clothes on him as well, for, the little fellow, who had clapped him on the back, explained, 'Sure the ither one'd have never fitted you again!' You may be sure that he was very grateful and thanked them a thousand times ('go raibh míle maith agat' as one says in Irish) and afterwards was often to be found on a fine summer evening sitting among the ruins, singing along with his friends.

News of Lusmore's cure travelled slowly through the local villages and eventually, some months later, a poor woman, whose son had a similar affliction, came to inquire about it. She was astounded to see Lusmore standing upright and tall and begged him to tell her how this came about. He was kind and sympathetic, explaining everything carefully, but warned her that the Sidhe were capricious and on no account to be offended.

She went away, full of hope, to fetch her son. However, he was a sour, spiteful fellow and when the Sidhe started to sing, instead of waiting quietly for a break as he had been told, he chimed in loudly and out of tune. The Little People were furious. They dragged him down among the stones, pinched and kicked him unmercifully, and as a crowning touch, clapped Lusmore's hump on top of his own, then chased him back along the road to his mother.

Sensible people keep away from the raths at night. A young man named Tomaseen Mike, tired out from cutting hay, fell asleep on one and when he awoke, found that a door had opened in the grass beside him, spilling out warm, golden light. Curious, he peered inside. There were the Little People enjoying a banquet. The table was covered with all kinds of enticing food and wine was poured from huge jugs into ivory and gold drinking horns. Suddenly a shout went up. Tomaseen had been seen! He was terrified, but although they dragged him swiftly into the rath, they spoke kindly and invited him to share the feast. He had slept so long that he had missed his evening meal and was only too delighted to join them.

The evening passed in a whirl of eating, drinking, singing and dancing. At length, Tomaseen thought he should be leaving. He had to rise early to milk the cows, so he thanked his kind hosts and departed. The door opened as he reached it and he found himself outside on the grass, gazing up at the night sky just paling into dawn. With some difficulty he plodded down the hill. He felt very stiff and found it hard to walk. He cut a stick from the hedge to support himself as he made his way home.

When he came to the farm, he stopped in amazement. Where there had been a neat, thatched, white-walled house with a clean, swept yard before it, there was only a pile of stones overgrown with nettles and brambles. By now he was very tired indeed and sat down to rest on a crumbling gatepost, totally bewildered. The sun rose as he sat there and presently along came a strangely dressed young lad in floppy blue trousers and a kind of long-sleeved tunic, flourishing a willow stick, driving up the cows for milking.

'Tell me, my young gossoon (boy),' called Tomaseen, 'is this the farm of Tómas Murphy?'

'Never heard of him, old man,' answered the lad carelessly.

Old man! The cheek of the child! Tomaseen slid down from the gatepost, determined to give the boy a scolding for his boldness, but somehow his legs gave away and fell on the dusty road. The farmer, who was following his son, helped him up and Tomaseen asked the same question.

'It was,' replied the man ,'but it must be over fifty years ago. The son of the house, Tomaseen Mike disappeared and there was nobody to care for the place after the old couple died. It is said he was taken by the Good People. I often heard my mother tell of it.'

'I am Tomaseen Mike,' said Tomaseen.

'God bless us!' exclaimed the farmer. 'Where have you been all these years? You'd best come home with me and tell us your story.'

When he came into the farm kitchen, Tomaseen caught sight of himself in a mirror. His face was pale and wrinkled, his hair white and his back bent with age. His banquet with the fairies had lasted fifty years. Tomaseen Mike was lucky. Some are said to have returned after such a feast to find that a hundred years had passed and nobody who knew of them was left.

Changelings

The Good People are also known to entice handsome young boys and pretty little girls to the rath and keep them as servants. They like to steal babies too and in the long ago days much thought was devoted to foiling this practice. Instead of the bonny child, the Gentry would leave 'Changelings', little yellow-faced, sickly, cranky creatures in the cradle. The human children were well treated in the rath, though some say that they were forever trying to make their way back to their own people, although, having entered the rath as babies, they were unaware of their true nature.

If you were unfortunate enough to be landed with a Changeling, it was quite a problem to get rid of it. One brave mother dangled the fairy child above a red-hot shovel. Afraid of being burned, it promptly wriggled out of her grasp, shot up the chimney and she found her own child on the hearthstone. Another method was to make the Changeling laugh. This was not so easy because in spite of looking like a baby, Changelings are incredibly old. They have seen, or think they have seen, everything in the world and the only way to make one laugh is to show it something it has not seen before.

Mrs Cronin found a little, shrivelled, black-eyed creature in her son's cot one day and fortunately realizing what had happened, went about getting rid of it at once. She hung a large pot of water above the turf fire in her kitchen. When it boiled, she went out to the henhouse, fetched a dozen eggs, broke them, threw the contents out into the yard, where the pigs enjoyed an unexpected treat, and put the shells in a bowl.

'What are you doing, Mammy?' asked the Changeling in its funny, creaky voice.

'Brewing, my son,' replied Mrs Cronin, throwing the eggshells into the cauldron.

'What are you brewing, Mammy?'

'Why, eggshells, of course!' she exclaimed.

The Changeling jumped up and down in the crib, shouting with laughter and clapping its hands.

'I'm fifteen hundred years in this world and I never saw eggshells brewed before!'

It laughed so much that it fell out onto the flagstones. A wind blew down the chimney, filling the room with smoke and when this cleared, her baby son, Liam, was back in the cot.

The Good People sometimes disagree. One young mother, grieving over the loss of her baby girl while she rocked the miserable, yellow-faced Changeling in the cradle, heard a tap at the door. Before she could open it, a small lady dressed in green came into the room. She wore a little red cap and carried a baby bundled in a green shawl so finely woven that no mortal could have made it. Her face was streaked with tears as she held out the child.

'Give me back my baby,' she begged.

'This is your baby? Of course, you can have him back.'

Delighted, the young woman handed over the Changeling. The fairy woman smiled as she hugged it and immediately its face lost the yellow colour, its dark hair curled all over its head and in her arms lay the prettiest, smallest baby you ever saw.

'I did not want him to go, but they took him while I was away,' she explained, all smiles, and vanished.

Needless to say the young woman was delighted to get her little girl back. Ever after she would leave a saucer of fresh milk on the windowsill at night for the Good People and the green shawl became a much valued family heirloom, for it had the power to lull even the most fractious baby to sleep.

The Sheerie

The Sheerie sounds like a solitary fairy but in reality the word is a collective noun for a group of little, baby-faced creatures, said to be the souls of unbaptized children trying to get back to life. They frequent old ruins, though not those of churches, standing stones, barrow type graves or hillocks and are visible at dusk, as small lights, flitting among the bushes, (be careful, not fireflies!) leading unwary travellers astray. These are wicked little people that you need to avoid. They seem to have a grudge against the living and delight in causing trouble.

They are, so we are told, to be found all over the country and amuse themselves with a strange kind of dark magic with which they cause humans to lose their wits and wander aimlessly through the night.

This is apparently done by singing on a high note that rings in the traveller's ears and after a little time, fills his head with sound and drives him crazy. He runs here and there, presumably trying to get rid of the noise, and can rush up and down a field, for an hour or more, fall into ditches or even, dangerously, over bridges into rivers, ending up exhausted when they grow bored with their fun and go in search of someone else to torment.

The Sheerie, as you can see, are bad news wherever they are seen and some folk say that the sight of them heralds a disaster of some kind or death, though this is more likely to be true of their relatives, the Water Sheerie.

The Water Sheerie

The Water Sheerie are probably more dangerous than the land Sheerie. They are not marsh gas, the 'Jacky Lantern' which makes a wavering, fitful, greenish light; theirs is golden and welcoming. They cluster together over the deepest parts of bogs, giving the appearance of a candlelit window, or perhaps a lantern, luring the lonely traveller to ask the way, or possibly seek a bed for the night. Woe betide the rambler who is caught out by their trick.

Martin O'Byrne nearly lost his life to them one spring evening as he searched for a lost cow. She was of the black Kerry breed and almost invisible standing against the furze bushes in the twilight.

He walked round his fields with a torch, calling 'come up, girl' and rattling a bucket but there was no sign of her. At length he went through the gate to the bog where he cut turf for his fire. He was not expecting to find her there, but having exhausted all the other places, decided to take just one look. He skirted round the edge calling, but saw nothing. Then, just as he was about to leave, a light flashed further out in the bog.

Thinking it was his neighbour he shouted, 'Did you see a cow at all, Sammy? I'm after missing one.'

There was no reply, but the light grew stronger and Martin began to think that maybe the cow was in the bog and his friend was trying to get her out, though he could not imagine why Sammy would not speak to him.

'I'm coming!' he cried and set off carefully, leaping from tussock to tussock until one gave away beneath his foot and he crashed full length into a bog hole.

Fortunately he managed to keep hold of his torch and waved it frantically.

'Sammy!' he shouted. 'I'm in the bog!'

The light did not move and there was no answer. Martin would have turned pale if he had not been covered in black bog mud. He held fast to a spindly bush and shouted again.

The light suddenly went out and he realized, cursing bitterly, that he had been fooled by the Water Sheerie. What was he to do now?

It was at that moment the battery in his torch died.

Just then, there was a loud sloshing noise accompanied by heavy breathing. A dark shape came slopping across the bog towards him. He could see its hunched shape against the twilight and gave himself up for lost. The monster came nearer—he closed his eyes.

A rough tongue licked his face, covering it with dribble and a rather startled 'Moo' rang in his ear—

It was his lost cow.

Martin made a grab for her tail, clung on and coaxed her to move away from the hole. Inch by inch, he dragged himself out and still clutching the tail, made his way back to the house. He was covered in black bog mud, as black as the cow herself but he was alive!

You may be sure that little Kerry cow was never sold and lived out her days in great comfort as the pet of the family.

Leprechauns

Leprechauns are usually old and grumpy, with long, white beards. Douglas Hyde, the first President of Ireland and a well-known translator of Irish poetry and legends tells us that the name in Irish is 'leath bróg', meaning 'one shoemaker', for he is usually seen working on only one shoe.

In the early 1900s, there was one such shoe exhibited in a glass case in the hallway of a house in the Southwest of Ireland. It was called 'the fairy shoe' and had been found by the small daughter of the family while playing on the hillside. 'A doll's shoe' some people would say scoffingly, but whoever saw a real leather doll's shoe so finely stitched and nailed with such tiny nails; the sole and heel worn down from walking and dancing?

Leprechauns keep their distance from the Sidhe and other groups of the Good People, though they make a lot of money selling shoes to them. This they hide away in various places and if you manage to catch a Leprechaun, hold tight and refuse to let him go until he tells you where he has hidden his crock of gold.

However, it is not so easy to capture these little men, for though they look elderly, they are wily, and as a last resort usually have a couple of stones within easy reach which they throw with great accuracy.

Brian McFee could testify to that. He was crossing the yard one dark, windy night with a bucket of oats for his horse when he heard the sound of hammering. He flashed his torch around but saw nothing. The noise seemed to come from the open door of the hayloft. These lofts are usually above the stables and are reached by a flight of stone steps up the side of the building so he climbed them as quietly as he could and peered in.

Comfortably ensconced on a cushion of hay, a little old man was tapping away at the heel of a shoe on the last held between his knees. The old fellow's mouth bristled with silver nails and Brian watched fascinated as he picked them out one by one and hammered them in. The sound was for all the world like the noise of a thrush tapping a snail on a stone to break the shell.

Brian had no thought of the crock of gold; he could have watched the little man all night but the wind caught his bucket and it clanged against the wall.

In an instant the Leprechaun turned and with amazing accuracy threw a couple of stones at him. One hit his torch, breaking the glass and bulb and the other knocked his hand so hard that he dropped the bucket. It rolled down the steps with hideous clanging and startled the horse which began to kick in its stall. By the time Brian had sorted himself out, and rubbed his bruises, the sprightly old fellow had disappeared.

Leprechauns are also known to carry an old-fashioned snuff box. If you are offered a pinch, do not try it, though they can be very courteous and persistent, for while you are helping yourself, the Leprechaun will throw the contents in your face and by the time you have recovered from your sneezing fit and mopped your streaming eyes, he will be far away.

Finbar O'Sullivan heard a tapping sound behind the hedge as he walked up one morning to see how his young cattle were doing. Peeping over it, he saw a Leprechaun in a green coat, red cap and leather apron sitting under a thorn tree, his last between his knees, hammering silver nails into the sole of a tiny scarlet slipper. Finbar knew exactly what to do. He walked quietly back along the path and struck off into the wood, moving very slowly, until he was just behind the little man. Then he pounced!

The Leprechaun gave a yell and tried to wriggle free, but Finbar had him by his beard and the seat of his grey worsted breeches and he could not move.

'Now, me maneen,' said Finbar. 'Tell me where you have your gold hid and I'll leave you go.'

'I will not, so!' shouted the Leprechaun, red in the face with fury.

'Then I'll keep aholt of you till you do!' said Finbar calmly.

The old fellow heaved and struggled, hissing with fury like a cat. Then he turned himself into a bird, then an eel, then a flaming stick, but through all the transformations, Finbar held on. At last, the exhausted little man pointed to a clump of ragwort.

'Leave me go. 'Tis there!' he shouted.

There was quite a lot of ragwort in that field, for Finbar was a lazy farmer, so he tied his red-spotted handkerchief round the plant as a marker and hurried home for a shovel.

Although he ran all the way, by the time he returned, every ragwort plant in the field sported a red-spotted handkerchief and the Leprechaun had vanished.

Long, long ago, a publican, walking from the town back to his village in the East of the country, sat down on a rock by the road to remove a stone from his boot. He shook it out and happening to look down, caught the eye of a little old Leprechaun, hiding in a clump of foxgloves beside him. Quick as a wink, he dropped the boot over him, scooped him up and held the top firmly closed.

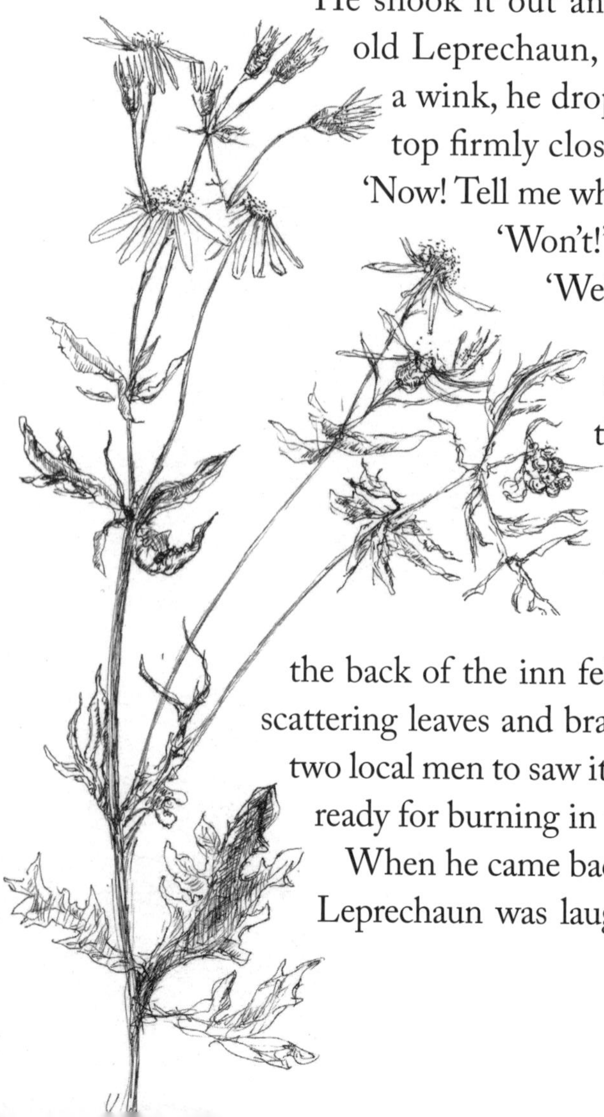

'Now! Tell me where you have your gold hid an' I'll leave you go,' he said.

'Won't!' came a voice from within the boot.

'Well, I'll keep you so!' replied the publican.

For the comfort of his unshod foot, he abandoned the road, returning home along the grass verge. Once there, he locked the Leprechaun in a wooden chest in his kitchen. Every day he asked the little fellow where was his gold and every day received the same reply. This went on for a year.

There was a great storm one night and a big tree at the back of the inn fell into the yard, crushing the wall around the yard and scattering leaves and branches everywhere. The publican was annoyed and paid two local men to saw it up with their long cross-cut saw, split and stack the logs ready for burning in the winter and clear up the mess.

When he came back into the kitchen after making these arrangements, the Leprechaun was laughing his head off inside the chest. The innkeeper was

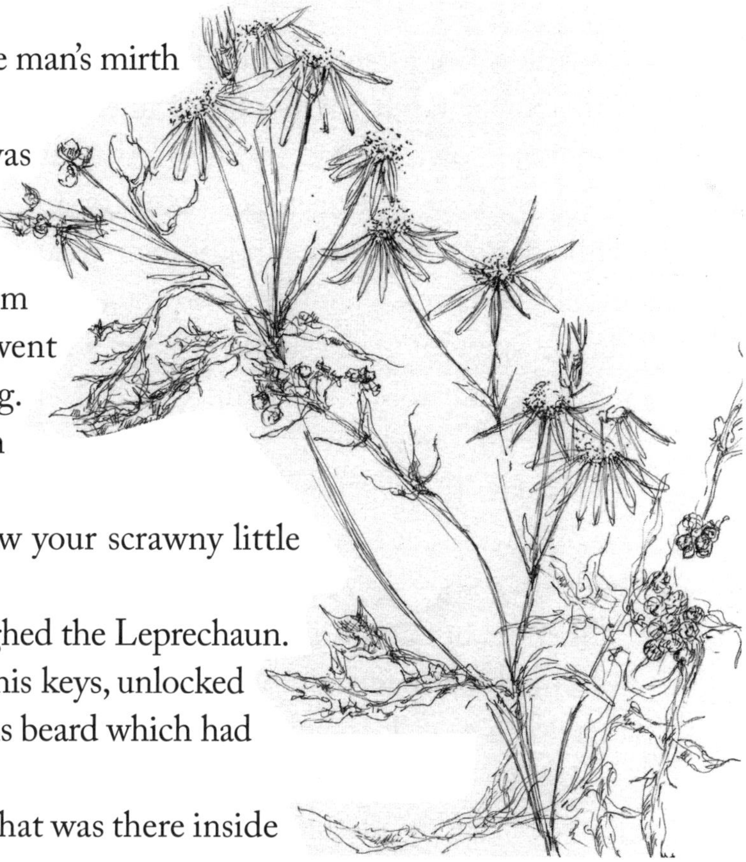

annoyed and asked the reason for the little man's mirth but got no answer.

A few months later, the Leprechaun was still stubborn and the publican just as stubborn. Neither would give an inch. The publican took some of his money from where he had hidden it in the well and went to the town to order hops for his brewing. On his return, he heard the Leprechaun laughing fit to burst.

'What's so funny?' he roared. 'I'll screw your scrawny little neck if you don't tell me!'

'I'm safe enough from that in here!' laughed the Leprechaun.

'No, you aren't!' The innkeeper fetched his keys, unlocked the chest and grabbed the little man by his beard which had grown long during his confinement.

'Now! Tell me! You laughed twice! What was there inside in the chest to make you laugh?'

The Leprechaun sniggered.

'The first time,' he said, 'was because inside the tree that fell was a big bag of gold money. 'Twas put there by a highwayman long ago an' he never came back for it because he was hanged! And you gave it to them two fellas! 'Tis enough to make a cat laugh!'

The innkeeper's face was purple with fury, 'Why, you—

'An' I'll tell you the rest,' said the little man hastily, fearing an explosion. 'I laughed today because there was a fella inside the stable watching ye getting the gold out of the well—'

The Leprechaun was flung unceremoniously onto the floor as the publican rushed out to see if his hoard was safe. You may be sure the little man lost no time in removing himself from the house, though he must have enjoyed the yells of fury echoing across the fields as the innkeeper discovered his money was gone.

Margaret O'Leary had better luck. Coming back from work over the hill one evening, she came upon a little shoemaker with his money spread out on his leather apron at the foot of a big rock. He was so busy counting it that he never noticed her as she whipped off her own apron and tied him up in it.

How he roared and screeched as she gathered up the gold pieces and ran off down the hill as fast as she could. History does not relate how the little man managed to untie himself, but she bought a fine farm with the money, married her sweetheart and was known far and wide for her generosity.

Others have not been so fortunate. One man who found a Leprechaun's crock while digging potatoes ran home in great glee only to find that the gold had turned into dead leaves, which is why some people say that if you find money anywhere, you should spend it at once, otherwise it will vanish.

An old lady told how she once saw a Leprechaun. She was out for a picnic, climbing a steep hill, head down, struggling along in the wake of her big brothers. It was a lovely day. The heather was in bloom and the scent of gorse was everywhere. There was no wind and the silence was only broken by the tiny cracking sound of furze buds breaking open in the hot sunlight.

She was hot and tired and wished her brothers would not walk so fast.

Something made her look up and there, beside a clump of heather, sat a little man in a green coat. His face was tanned and a leather-wrapped bundle lay by his side.

Thrilled and fascinated, she opened her mouth to call the others but with an impish smile he shook his head and laid a finger to his lips as much as to say 'this is our secret'.

She smiled back, suddenly very happy, and nodded. Just then her brothers shouted at her to hurry up, so with a little wave, she walked on.

Although she looked carefully on her way down, he was gone but she never forgot him, although she was over eighty when she told the story.

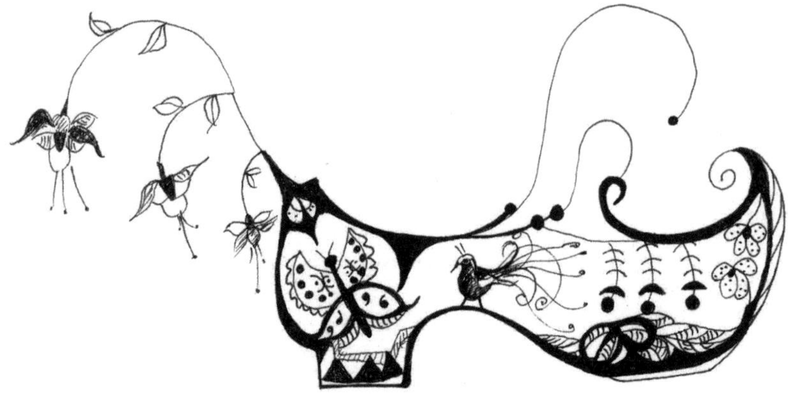

The Red Man

The Red Man (*Fear dearg* in Irish), so called from his red cap and coat, is another of the solitary fairies and not one you would care to meet. He frequents lonely roads at night, graveyards and other such places.

Danny Carroll was returning from the pub late one cloudy April night. As he passed beneath the churchyard wall, he heard the sound of digging and hoisted himself up to see what was going on.

He could dimly make out a figure and called, 'Hello Tim, you're working late! Is there a funeral tomorrow?'

The dark shape waved an arm seeming too puffed to speak, so Danny jumped down and went towards it.

Just then the clouds drew away from the face of the moon, and Danny saw the red cap, the glint of two bright, piggy eyes beneath it, and the heavy red coat. It was the Red Man.

His knees knocked together in fright, and he could hardly stand. He tried to run, but found himself frozen to the ground.

The Red Man laughed. 'This fella,' he said, gesturing at the grave, 'is after being put in the wrong churchyard, so he must be moved to Kilknock. Dig him up and take him there an' if that's his final resting place, I'll let ye go.'

Danny dug at speed. He could not wait to get away. The coffin was soon uncovered, and with great difficulty, he carried it down the two miles of dusty road that led to Kilknock. The

Red Man led him to a huge blackberry bush from the midst of which loomed a leaning tombstone.

'In here!' he said tersely.

Danny protested that he had no scythe to cut away the brambles, but before the words were out of his mouth, the tool fell at his feet.

'Now!' snarled the Red Man.

With the thought that after this he could get away from the terrible being pacing up and down behind him, chewing loudly on something that cracked—like—like what?—like a bone?—whose bone?—a human bone?—Danny dug like man possessed.

By the time he had pushed the coffin into its new grave, He could hardly hold the shovel and sweat was pouring off him like water. He mopped his forehead and turned to go but a strong hand seized his arm.

'Not so fast, me manneen,' whispered the Red Man. 'I'm after thinking that 'tisn't here at all the coffin should be. Ballyross might be the place, so up with it an' we'll try again.'

The same thing happened at Ballyross and at Kilbogue. By this time Danny was practically crawling down the road.

At Dunmore, he only had the strength to excavate a shallow hole and as he was putting in the coffin, he heard a cock crow in a neighbouring farm and lifting his eyes, saw first light on the horizon. The chill little wind that comes with dawn swirled around him, blowing dust from the grave into his face. He turned and saw that the Red Man had vanished.

'Begor' Herself'll kill me,' said Danny to himself, as he staggered wearily home, ''tis the last time ever I stay late at the pub! I'm destroyed, so I am.'

Indeed, he looked so tired and wretched when he staggered into the house and told his story that he got a fine big breakfast instead of a telling-off.

Padraig Sweeney was not so lucky. He was the town drunk, well known for spending all his money on whiskey and porter. His poor wife was left to look after their farm and care for a brood of children on half nothing while Padraig strolled into town like a gentleman and spent the day propping up the bar in Cassidy's pub.

His friends were few but he could usually manage to wheedle a pint out of any stranger who dropped in and on the day of the annual festival when the priest came down to the pier to bless the fishing boats, there was a *ceilidh*, (dancing, singing and story-telling). That evening, He went from pub to pub (and there were plenty of pubs in Irish towns at the time), swallowing as many unattended drinks as he could find and weaving his way out before anyone noticed him.

When he decided to go home the trouble started. His legs seemed to want to go back to town, while his head and arms set off for the farm. He fell heavily onto the road and sat up, cursing.

'Me poor man, are ye not well?' asked a voice.

'Not well…' echoed Padraig, looking up at a very short, stout fellow who stood beside him, dressed in a red cap and coat.

'Come along. Ye could do with a rest I see,' said the stranger.

A strong arm heaved the drunkard to his feet, and they progressed through the town in a series of swoops until they came to the church.

The Red Man, for of course it was he, up to his tricks again, pushed open the door of the side chapel.

'There's a fine soft bed in there for ye. Lie down there an' rest yourself aisy,' he murmured, as he propelled Padraig through the doorway with a hefty kick in the backside.

He took care not to step inside though, for the Good Folk will never enter a church or stay in a place where there is a priest.

Padraig tottered in, tripped and landed on what he thought was a bed. It seemed very narrow, but the middle part was soft and he was soon snoring away.

In the morning, waking with a sore head, he found himself lying on the corpse of old Mrs Mullins, whose funeral was scheduled for that day. He leaped up with a loud scream, wondering how he had got there and ran terrified out into the churchyard, sure that her ghost was pursuing him

It was raining and as he staggered home, he heard someone laughing behind his back, but however many times he turned in fury to see who was there, the road remained empty and the laughter got louder.

Did he sign the pledge after that? He did not, more shame to him! But the drink got to him in the end. Not long after, for he tripped going home one night and hit his head off a stone in the ditch. Maybe the Red Man had him after all; it is not for me to say.

The Grey Man

The Grey Man (*Fear liath* in Irish) most often seen in the mountains or along the coast. He might best be described as a malevolent mist, for nobody can say exactly what he looks like. Indeed you might wonder whether he is a member of the fairy tribe at all, for those who have glimpsed him describe him as swathed in a floating grey cloak, which conceals him completely.

Others have seen a grey face and a pair of large, mournful eyes, but this sighting was by a holiday visitor unfamiliar with the countryside, and after exhaustive questioning turned out to be a white cow looking over a hedge on a misty day. Without doubt, the Grey Man is a nasty being. He delights in throwing unexpected blankets of fog over the sea and his misty cloak writhes and shakes though he were laughing when this causes trouble to mankind.

In the Blasket Islands there was a superstition that if you went down to the seashore on a certain day, you would disappear into the mist. There was no mention of the Grey Man but it sounds as if he might have been somewhere about. Perhaps it was considered bad luck to mention his name, as it often is when not-so-nice members of the Gentry are around.

However, the following incident occurred on the mainland coast. It was a perfect day for fishing when the *Mary Kate* sailed out. The sun shone, there was a light breeze and the crew laughed and joked as they heaved the net, moving slowly across the water towards the mouth of the bay, as it paid out behind them.

They had been out for an hour and were just beginning to haul in when a blanket of fog came up from behind them and in two minutes everything outside the boat had vanished. It was so sudden that for a moment everyone stood staring, then the Mate ran for the foghorn and the men continued hauling in the net as fast as they could, while the Master checked the compass and proceeded slowly ahead.

There seemed to be no sign of a break. The wind had dropped as often happens with such mists and although this made no difference to them because of the engine, he ordered a lantern to be hoisted at the masthead. It seemed that they were not going to make port that evening unless conditions improved, and he was concerned as to whether they had enough fuel to take them into the open sea where they could heave to for the night and return home again next morning.

It was then that they heard the unmistakable sound of breaking waves, a sound well known to all coastal sailors. Somehow they had come too close to the shore. The Master rushed to the wheel and swung it hard over, away from the danger, but he was too late. The boat struck the chain of rocks known as 'The Cobbles' and a great hole was stove in her side.

John Coffey, a local farmer, driving his cows home along the clifftop, heard the crash as the *Mary Kate* foundered on The Cobbles and recognizing the sound, although he could see nothing because of a strange patch of mist, ran to the village and raised the alarm.

The younger men were out fishing, but there were some elderly seamen who knew very well what was needed and gathered crews from among the wives who could handle an oar, the doctor, the priest and several strong lads, only too pleased to be hauled out of school. All of them remarked on the patch of mist that lay like a writhing cloud around The Cobbles and nowhere else on the bay but by the time they reached the wreck, it had vanished.

The *Mary Kate's* crew, huddled dripping on the rocks, all swore that they had heard the sound of someone laughing but when the mist cleared, there was nobody there. The Master and crew were convinced that the accident was caused by the Grey Man, but you do not write that on an insurance claim form!

The Grey Man is also said to sour milk as he passes. Sceptics will say that this is caused by thunder in the air, but in days long ago a busy woman might leave a bucket of fresh milk in the dairy, intending to put it through the separator later and return to find it souring. If she went into the yard, she might notice a patch of mist drifting up the boreen away from the farm. But that could be smoke from someone's fire, couldn't it?

Another habit of the Grey Man is to blacken the potatoes as he goes by. This was serious mischief in a country that relied on the crop. Even among all the modern ideas and innovations in Ireland today, some folk still believe in him.

An American friend on holiday in Kerry offered to fetch a bucket of spuds from the clamp, an oblong heap of earth by the byre wall where layers of the season's potatoes, interspersed with layers of soil, were stored against the winter, covered with an old tarpaulin. She brought back a pair of rosary beads as well.

'Look what I've found! Someone must have lost their beads,' she said and was amazed when the son of the house said, 'Oh, no, 'tis against the Grey Man,' and ran out to replace them in the clamp.

The Dullahan

The Dullahan is most often seen at the time of fairy festivals, May Eve, Midsummer and Hallowe'en. He is the Irish version of the headless horseman, cantering across the country on a wild black stallion, black cloak flying, but the difference is that he actually *carries* his head which glows in the dark and lights the way for him. It is a weird sight to see the headless body upright in the saddle, one hand on the reins, carrying the head in the other, like a lantern, or hanging it at his saddle bow as he picks his way down overgrown paths.

By holding up the head, the Dullahan can see who is about to die, even from far across the county. He gallops to the house and the head shouts out the name of the person to draw the soul out. Those who are unwise enough to look from the window on hearing the noise are often temporarily blinded.

Sometimes the Dullahan appears as a headless coachman, driving a pair of black horses with a coffin clearly visible in the coach. The horses snort fire and their hooves strike sparks from the ground, yet they make no sound. Instead of a Banshee, in certain families, the headless coachman and his team is said to herald a death. Strangely enough, it does not seem to matter where a member of that family dies. The coachman appeared one night at a certain house near Dublin. The family in question was bewildered, as nobody had died or was even ill. It was not until several weeks later that they learned of the passing of an uncle in Australia.

Not so long ago, Ritchie O'Brien, returning from visiting a neighbour saw the Dullahan sitting on his horse at a level crossing. Fired with courage after a few jars of poteen,

he asked the apparition what it was doing there. The Dullahan held up the greenish glowing head. Its eyes were bright and black and knowing; its mouth a dark cavern 'waiting for the souls'. It shouted the names of three local people.

'They will all come tonight,' it breathed.

'Oh! Oh!' shuddered Ritchie, 'well—er—er—good evening, sir—er—, my lord.'

He passed on as fast as he could without running, for fear of being chased, surrounded by the stench of the horrible head's breath and hoping with all his heart that the Dullahan was not following him.

Later that night a train crashed into a lorry crossing the tracks, and those named were killed.

The Lennan Shee

The Lennan Shee is a beautiful fairy woman. She entices young men to fall in love with her. If they do not, she becomes their slave, hoping to win them that way. If they do become infatuated, she draws upon their life force until they waste away and die. She has been called the Muse of poets and musicians; those she inspires live brilliant though short lives.

Darragh Flynn was such a man. He came of a very musical family. There was always someone playing the fiddle or the pipes or singing in the house.

He himself played the flute and composed wonderful songs. His melodies were simple but haunting and the words of his songs lingered in your head for days. He was often seen walking in the hills or by the lake, humming to himself and beating time with his blackthorn stick

One day at the lakeside he met a woman wrapped in the usual black shawl, walking along the path with her basket. 'Good day, ma'am,' he said, having been brought up to greet people politely whether he knew them or not.

The woman did not answer and passed on. Her shawl was pulled so far over her face that he could not see it and thought it strange that she did not speak to him, but concluded that she was visiting in the area, since any of the local women would know him well.

The next day he went up the mountain and coming down passed her again and again greeted her, though she still did not respond. That night, as they sat around the turf fire after supper, he asked if there were any strangers staying in the village. His parents and sisters said there was nobody but his youngest brother, a lad of twelve years, said that he had seen the back of a young woman going along by the lake a day or two ago. It was definitely a stranger, for being a sharp young fellow, he knew everyone in the area, backview or front. They pondered on it for a while and then the talk turned to other things and the strange woman was forgotten.

Not, however, by Mairead, the little servant girl, who worshipped Darragh Flynn from afar, although he took very little notice of her, except to ask her for a cup of tea if he was thirsty. Mairead was determined to find out who the strange woman was. She had a feeling that the intruder was somehow up to no good.

The next time Darragh saw the strange woman, she was standing on the bridge where the lake flowed into the river.

'Good evening, ma'am,' he said, as he passed and decided to 'chance his arm', as they say, 'Are ye staying long in these parts?'

The woman turned, startled, for the noise of the water had covered the sound of his footsteps, the shawl fell back from her head, and he drew a breath of amazement. She was the most wonderful creature he had ever seen; her long auburn hair fell round a face so beautiful that his heart leapt. She regarded him from eyes the colour of Kerry violets that grow in the bogs.

'That might depend…' she said softly.

'On what?' he asked.

'On yourself, Darragh Flynn,' she replied. 'I have gifts for you—if you will take them.'

'Gifts?' croaked the young man.

'Gifts,' she repeated firmly. 'You may meet me by the lake tomorrow if you will. I must be away now.'

She turned on her heel and walked off, leaving him staring.

Darragh Flynn ate no supper that night. He spent his time sitting in the chimney corner, staring at the flames of the turf fire and humming quietly under his breath. The family were well used to this.

'Sure, leave him be,' said his mother. 'He's after composing a song. Ye'll get no good out of him till 'tis done.'

Mairead watched him from the back kitchen as she washed up the pots and pans. He seemed excited and presently went out into the yard where she could hear him walking up and down.

The next morning, he bolted his breakfast and away off with him down to the lake. He stayed there all day but the beautiful woman never came. This went on for a week and he spoke little and seemed tired as though he had not slept.

Then she came.

Mairead watched them from the bedroom window, walking along the narrow path, heads close together.

Darragh came back that evening elated with a wild look in his eye and sat by the fire whistling and playing scraps of airs on his flute.

The next day he was at the lake again but the lady never came. The day after that she was there and they walked together up the mountain to the old caves that were said to be where the last of the Firbolgs had lived, the small dark men, who originally inhabited Ireland before the Tuatha Dé Danaan conquered them.

After that, no two days were the same. Darragh was out roving the countryside with the strange lady, or slumped in the chimney corner playing strange, wild airs they had never heard before. He grew thin and pale, seldom slept and ate little. It was as if a fire were burning him up from inside.

His mother was worried; her father had died of the dreaded tuberculosis and she was mortally afraid that Darragh had contracted it. She made all kinds of tempting food for him, but after a few mouthfuls he would spring to his feet and rush out of the door as though he had heard a voice calling him.

'Leave him be, he'll come right,' said the father.

But he did not and Mairead also began to be worried. Winter was setting in; it was cold and damp for walking by the lake or scrambling on the mountain.

Mairead was given a day off to visit her parents before the bad weather set in, but instead she went round the lake to visit her Granny and returned very quiet, with a solemn face. The farmer's wife put it down to homesickness and was especially kind to her.

Soon afterwards, one night, when the family was out playing cards at a neighbour's house and Darragh dozed uneasily on the old settle by the fire, Mairead stole out to the stable. From a tin on the shelf, she took several rusty old iron nails and as Darragh slept, she ripped the hem of his coat and then sewed it up again with the nails inside.

The next day, when he was seeking the lady, the little servant girl followed. She saw the woman standing by the water. It was cold but sunny and her wonderful hair lay across the black shawl on her shoulders like a fire.

As Darragh walked up to her she turned, the uttered a screech that stood the hair on Mairead's head.

'What have you done?' she screamed.

Darragh was startled. 'Why, nothing,' he answered.

'You did—you did!—an' I nearly had ye!' she shrieked again.

Before his eyes she suddenly changed into the most repulsive hag he had ever seen and with a last despairing yell, jumped into the lake.

For a long time Darragh stood staring out across the grey water, then turned for home with tears running down his face and saw Mairead.

The girl had watched, thunderstruck, as the lady transformed and was still rooted to the ground with terror.

'What are you doing here? What have you done?' he asked furiously.

''Twas the Lennan Shee,' she replied boldly, 'She had you in thrall. I sewed iron nails into your coat, the way me Granny told me an' ye saw her as she truly is.'

Darragh was furious. He grabbed her by the collar, marched her home and complained her bitterly to his mother. That lady was delighted and took no notice of his ranting. She gave Mairead six silver pennies and the most of a week off at Christmas in gratitude for her cleverness.

Darragh seemed to have forgotten the hideous hag who had jumped into the lake and often spoke of his beautiful lady. He completely ignored Mairead, but the rest of the family were thankful that his life had been spared and could not have been kinder. Still, she was sad and felt that she had somehow done wrong but as time went on and his songs brought him fame and renown, he forgave her and when she married his younger brother, the music he played at the wedding would have caused a lame cow to get up and dance.

The Banshee

The Banshee, from the Irish '*bean*' (woman) and '*sidhe*', is a fairy woman usually attached to one or other of the ancient Irish families like the O'Neills, O'Connors and O'Gradys. She is heard wailing and crying just before a member of that family dies, but is in no way malevolent.

She may appear like a tall, pale woman dressed in white with a black cloak, weeping and lamenting, wringing her hands as she walks round the house but if you are brave enough to venture outside, she disappears and only the sound of her sobbing is heard.

If the person who died is particularly well known, more than one Banshee will turn up to wail at his passing. The sound of their mournful cries is audible even inside the house, echoing through the passages and even into the sick-room itself, where, if the patient has not already expired, the eerie tones are certainly enough to assist him speedily on his way.

The 'keen' (Irish *caoineadh*), which women all over the country used to raise at funerals until the last century, is said to be an imitation of the Banshee's cry.

The Skegashee

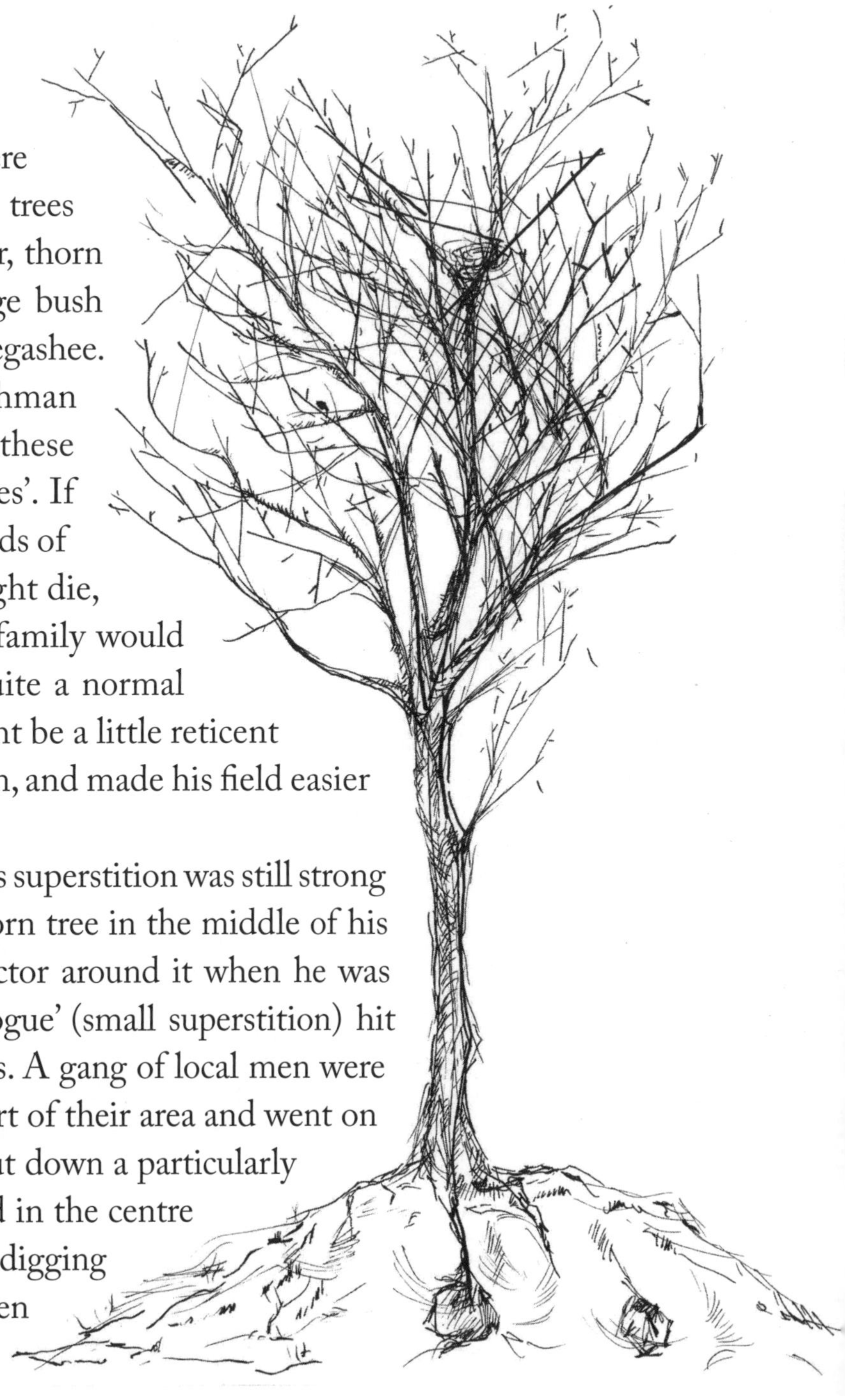

The Skegashee is a tree spirit. *Sceach* in Irish means an isolated tree. They are found everywhere in Ireland where there are often single trees in fields or at roadsides, frequently elder, thorn or rowan. Sometimes a particularly large bush standing alone may be the home of a Skegashee.

Not so long ago, no right-minded Irishman would dream of cutting down one of these trees, which were regarded as 'fairy trees'. If you were foolish enough to do so, all kinds of ill-luck would befall you. Your cows might die, you could lose all your money or your family would fall ill. The solitary tree was, in fact, quite a normal sight in Ireland, though the farmer might be a little reticent in explaining why he had not cut it down, and made his field easier to cultivate.

At the end of the twentieth century, this superstition was still strong among countryfolk. A farmer with a thorn tree in the middle of his field would carefully manoeuvre his tractor around it when he was ploughing or reaping. Indeed the 'pishogue' (small superstition) hit the headlines of the national newspapers. A gang of local men were employed to build a motorway across part of their area and went on strike when the foreman told them to cut down a particularly fine blackthorn tree. It would have stood in the centre of the highway if they had continued digging and levelling in the direction they had been told to go, so they stopped work.

The foreman was not from that part of the country. He laughed incredulously at them, but the men were adamant. They sat down on the side of the ditch and refused to continue.

The foreman was infuriated. He pulled out his mobile phone and rang his superior, almost incoherent with rage, spluttering about 'uneducated, superstitious louts' and wondering if this was not a ploy to get a rise in wages. The man in charge laughed, but when he heard that the workers were serious about it, he rather nervously rang Head Office. Fortunately his boss was a countryman himself and understood the problem immediately. 'Tell them to go round it,' he said.

So somewhere in the Midlands, a very fine blackthorn tree stands on a curve in the road. One wonders what the Skegashee thinks of all the cars.

The Merrow

The Merrow is the Irish mermaid or merman. They are said to be found along the wilder coasts and fishermen hate to see them because they foretell a strong gale. Farmers with land running down to the shore have reported Merrows coming out of the waves at dusk in the shape of small, hornless or 'polly' cows, and wandering about the fields grazing the salty grass.

Male mermen are not handsome. They have green faces, green teeth and eyes like a pig. However, to make up for it, they are very amiable. Denis Casey, a farmer in Galway was quite friendly with one.

Denis had a small farm by the sea, with a stream of fresh water running into the bay below. He eked out his meagre earnings by distilling poteen in an old boat shed by the shore. Now, as everyone knows, you need pure water to make the mash and a lonely place to distil the spirit, if you are not to be caught doing it. If you are, the fine is stiff, not to mention the fact that you will lose your still and other equipment. Denis's site was ideal and his brew particularly good.

One day, as he walked along the strand, he was hailed by a merman wearing a red cocked hat and sitting on a rock a few feet from shore.

'Denis Casey, Denis Casey,' he called. 'Would you give us a sup of your poteen? I hear it 'tis the finest in Ireland!'

'I will, an' welcome,' replied Denis. 'Will you come ashore?'

'I will not,' said the Merrow, 'but let you bring it out to me an' I'll see you right!'

Much amused by the ugly fellow, Denis waded out with a bottle wondering whether his payment might be in fish or lobsters. When he reached the rock, the Merrow took a good swig and smiled delightedly, showing all his strange green teeth. Grabbing Denis by the arm, he slithered off the rock and bore the startled farmer down to the bottom of the sea.

They landed in a patch of white sand planted with seaweeds in different colours, for all the world like a garden. The merman led him up the path bordered with scallop shells to a neat little house made from coloured stones and timbers of wrecked ships. Inside, the merman hung his cocked hat on a peg by the door and ushered Denis into what he called his 'treasure room' telling him to choose what he liked. There were all manner of beautiful and costly things from wrecked ships scattered about; heaps of jewels and gold, porcelain and pottery in many shapes and colours, furniture, even a bicycle and a set of lobster pots. Denis looked in surprise at the lobster pots.

'What's them doin' here?' he asked. 'Surely ye'd do better to set them above, round the rocks off the headland?'

He peered at them. 'Why, there's somethin' inside! Whatever is it?' For he could see vague, blue, misty shapes weaving about behind the willow sticks of the lobster pots.

'Them's the souls of drowned sailors, me bucko,' answered the merman. 'They do be roamin' around outside, sobbin' someth' pitiful. Keeps me awake of nights it do, so I collected 'em up an' they do stay a bit quieter when they're together.'

'They wants to get home to the shore,' Denis told him. 'They can't rest easy till they gets a proper burial in the ground. They do be land creatures for all they goes on the sea,' explained Denis. 'If it's all right by your Honour, I'll take them as me payment.'

The merman was much surprised at Denis's choice. 'Sure, there's no value in them!' he exclaimed.

'No,' answered Denis, 'only that I couldn't rest easy in the bed myself, knowing they was down here crying to get home.'

'You're a good an' kindly man,' said the merman. 'Come away now an' I'll help you to shore with them.'

He produced a second cocked hat which he stuck on the farmer's head and together they rose up through the water carrying the lobster pots.

As soon as Denis reached shore, he piled the pots in his shed and set off to see the priest, who was amazed at the story.

The next day, the whole village turned out for the sailors' funeral. Many families had lost relatives to the sea and were glad to show their respect for these unknown souls. So now the wandering sailors rest in a small, windblown graveyard by the sea, lobster pots and all, with a fine headstone to remember them by.

As Denis was returning from the burial, he felt something heavy in his coat pocket. He put in his hand and drew out a bag of gold coins. Whether they were from the Merrow or the sailors nobody knows, but after that everything he did prospered and he still went on making the finest poteen in Ireland.

Merrow women, in spite of their fishtails and webbed fingers are very beautiful, with green eyes and long golden hair streaming from under their little red caps. Some people up in the West say that it is not a cap but a cape that the female Merrows wear. Frank Delaney knew all about that. He had a fine little fishing boat. Taking her out of harbour one evening to haul up his lobster pots, he heard a woman crying and saw a Merrow sitting on the end of a the chain of rocks that marked the headland. Presently he cut his engine and drifted past her. She was the most beautiful woman he had ever seen and he longed to have her for a wife.

'What ails you, ma'am?' he asked.

'I'm after losing me cape,' she sighed, 'and as well you know I can't go home
to the bottom of the sea without it.'

Frank was already besotted with her. 'Come into the boat an' we'll go searching,' he suggested.

The Merrow declined, but condescended to swim along beside him.

Frank picked up the first float on his line and hauled the pot up into the boat. He picked out the lobster from inside, catching it carefully behind the big claws and dropped it into a box. Three more fine specimens followed, but draped round the fifth, was what looked like a piece of old tarpaulin.

Frank suspected it might be what they were looking for and hastily shoved it in among the lobsters, re-baited the pots and put them out again.

The Merrow was looking very downcast and he persuaded her to come to his cottage for the night and they would resume the search in the morning. She agreed and when he had seated her in his kitchen—not too near the fire, she begged—he took the lobsters round the side of the house and stuffed the cape up into the rafters of the shed where he kept his fishing gear and a small boat.

The Merrow was sad that she could not go home, but eventually she settled down with Frank and they had two children, a handsome boy and a pretty little girl with long golden hair like her mother's. She became friendly with the other women in the village, but could often be seen sitting on the headland, gazing out to sea with a wistful expression on her face.

One day, there was a terrible gale. Trees blew down, lumps of thatch were torn off roofs and loose articles such as buckets and nets ended up in a tangled pile at the bottom of the street.

In the midst of it all, there was a mighty crash—Frank's shed blew down.

The family rushed out to rescue what they could, helped by their neighbours. The boat was intact, but the lobster pots were flattened and broken. The Merrow hauled them out from beneath the remains of the roof and among them found a long, dark green piece of material that looked like a tarpaulin.

'Frank! How could you!' she cried.

He looked up and seeing what she held, blushed crimson and looked guilty.

''Twas the way I couldn't let you go—,' he muttered. 'You were the most beautiful woman I ever seen—or ever will see—. Don't, ah don't go away from me now. Think of the children!'

The Merrow looked at her little family. Was there a hint of a tear in her sea-green eyes?

'I won't leave ye for ever. I'll come back,' she said, wrapping the cape round her shoulders and ran down to the shore, where she vanished into the waves.

Frank was heartbroken and the children pined but the Merrow kept her promise. She often came back to visit them, and on fine days you would see them picnicking on the strand. But she was always careful to hide her cape somewhere safe before she swam ashore.

The Pooka

The Pooka frequents lakesides, particularly those which lie dark and solitary among the hills. He takes the shape of a beautiful black horse, with a shining coat and silver- mounted bridle. The lone angler is most likely to meet him but woe betide the man who tries to catch him. The moment his rein is grabbed, the unfortunate captor's hand freezes to the leather. He cannot let go and the Pooka jumps into the lake, carrying his prize down to his house in the depths. Sometimes, if he is feeling particularly skittish, he will allow himself to be mounted, then takes off across country at top speed. No matter how the rider seeks to control him or to dismount he cannot escape, and vanishes into the lake with the Pooka.

There is a lake somewhere in Ireland, one end of which never freezes, even in the hardest winter. The reason for it is this:

Molly O'Rourke was a pretty young girl who lived on a remote farm in the hills. Every so often, in hot summers when the well was low, she would come to draw water from the lake. The Pooka saw her and fell in love. He determined to make her his wife.

The next time she brought her buckets to the lakeshore he trotted up to her. She had never seen such a fine beast before. 'You must be some rich man's horse,' she said, 'I'll bring you up to our stable till we find out who owns you.'

The Pooka obligingly stood still while she scrambled onto his back, but once she was settled, away he went into the lake with her.

Molly did not think much of the Pooka's house. Although beautifully ornamented with freshwater pearls, shells and water-weeds, it was cold and rather damp. She did not think much of the raw fish and snails that he offered her either. Though, mind you, he was very kind and did all he could to please her.

'What we need is a chimney,' she said one day. 'Can ye not go and find Dan Dillon and get him to build one?'

The Pooka willingly trotted off, and returned with Dan Dillon the mason, who built them a grand chimney, and was well rewarded for his trouble.

Because of the Pooka's chimney, that end of the lake never froze. Molly cooked bastable bread (traditional Irish soda bread baked in an iron pot) and good fish stews, which the Pooka enjoyed and they lived happily for many a year.

And how did the fire keep going under water? Ah, go on away with you, that's the Pooka's magic. You can believe it or not.

Prince O'Donoghue

Others beside the Pooka live under the water—one of them is the great prince O'Donoghue, once ruler of all the land surrounding the town of Killarney. He walked out upon the waters of nearby Loch Leane one day, watched in amazement by all his court and slowly sank beneath the waves to claim a new kingdom. Folk say that ever after, on each May Day morning, he rises up and takes a stroll through his old domain. The descendants of Willie Doody, who lived in the area in the eighteenth century, certainly believed it.

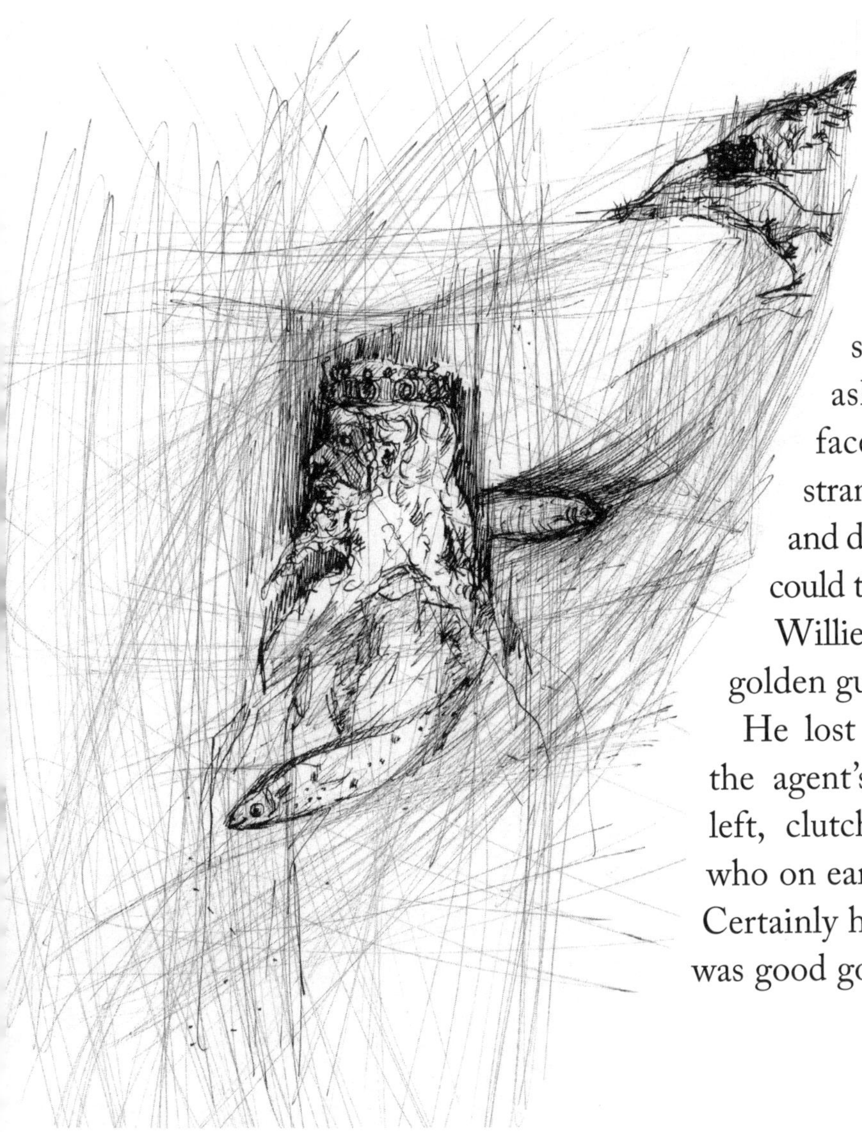

Willie was sitting by the lake on May Day morning, pondering sadly on the impossibility of gathering enough money to pay the rent of his little farm to Lord Kenmare's agent. Suddenly, he was tapped on the shoulder by a tall, very strangely dressed gentleman, who asked the reason for his melancholy face. On hearing the problem, the stranger tossed a purse in Willie's lap and disappeared before the startled farmer could thank him.

Willie peered into the purse. It was full of golden guineas!

He lost no time in presenting himself at the agent's house, paid what he owed and left, clutching the receipt, still wondering who on earth his benefactor could have been. Certainly his dress was strange but his money was good golden guineas. Perhaps some of the rich landowners, who lived around the lake, had guests from foreign parts staying for the fishing.

Still pondering on the stranger, Willie headed for home.

The agent, returning to his office some time later, opened his desk to get a pen. There, instead of the money he had placed in it, lay a pile of golden gingerbread, each piece stamped with the head of George IV, the king of England at the time. The agent swore, but there was nothing he could do. Willie was back on the farm with the receipt in his pocket.

From that time onwards, everything prospered for Willie and his family, and he was often heard to bless the day he met with O'Donoghue from under the water.

A Cluricaun

Cluricauns

Cluricauns look similar to Leprechauns, but stouter, with fat, rosy faces. They live solitary lives in cellars, because they are very fond of 'the drink'.

Of course, the cellar has to be well stocked, so in olden days they were mostly found in the houses and castles of the rich and powerful, where their small depredations went unnoticed. They seem to have discarded the usual fairy dress in favour of the clothes most usually worn in such places at the time – tricorne hats, knee breeches and brocaded coats with lace ruffles, no doubt heavily ornamented with wine stains. One wonders whether this was some zany idea dreamed up to permit them to mingle with guests attending a party and get a free meal with all trimmings, or whether they developed delusions of grandeur from living in such exalted surroundings.

They are also known to help themselves to food. Many a cook has looked round for the jug of cream or the tartlet she has just put on the table behind her, only to find it gone and nobody in the kitchen who might have taken it.

Cluricauns are fond of giving parties themselves. They would entertain their friends with the best wine and often closed the evening on a wild ride by moonlight, perched on the back of the Master's sheep or goats. Unfortunately the amount consumed in these revels could not be overlooked, and the servants were blamed, but they mostly took it in good part for if, at other times, the Master enquired about missing bottles, which they had purloined, they were able to blame the Cluricaun.

Nowadays, with the decline of the great houses, the difficulty in finding staff and the modern trend for eating out, rather than entertaining at home, they have almost disappeared as indeed, alas, have most of the cellars. Somehow Cluricauns do not fit in with the serried ranks of bottles in the wine shops today, but they may have emigrated. The wine estates in France are just the place for them, and if you go wine-tasting and keep your eyes open, you may just see a bibulous little face peering at you round a barrel.

The Grogoch

The Grogoch is well known in the North of Ireland. For some reason best known to himself, he has never been seen in the South. Indeed it is said that he emigrated from Scotland and perhaps prefers to stay in the North of this country.

His English equivalent is the Brownie and like him, he helps around the house but there the resemblance ends, for the Grogoch has no clothes. He is covered all over in ginger hair and although he does not look very prepossessing, he is gentle and kind.

His one idea is to help in the house or on the farm and he never seems to tire of work, in fact he is a workaholic. Although he has the fairy gift if invisibility, he can sometimes be seen in the fields at harvest time, working away in the blazing sunshine, even when the rest of the men are lying in the shade under the hedge eating their lunches. Indeed he will occasionally come and pull them by the shirt to try and get them back to work.

Rosie McCabe had a Grogoch who lived in a cave among a clump of rocks on the top of the hill behind the farm. He helped her around the house. Apart from being annoyed when he woke her in the early morning, banging and clattering as he cleaned out the kitchen range, brought in wood and turf for the fire and water from the spring, she was pleased to have him.

It was pleasant to come down to a clean, warm kitchen with the fire crackling and the kettle on the boil. She never knew how he managed to light the stove, for he did not seem to understand about matches, but that was no matter. He would watch the bread rising before the hearth for her, and come to tug at her skirt when it was ready to go into the oven; he even rocked the baby in the cradle when he cried and carried baskets of laundry to hang on the line. Her buckets of drinking water were never empty and he did all the washing up, although sometimes he was clumsy and broke things.

That year they had a glut of plums in the orchard. The Grogoch was in his element, collecting great basketfuls, which he brought into the house for preserving or making into jam. He washed the jam crocks and kept an eye on the pan in case it boiled over. He was everywhere round the kitchen and got under Rosie's feet, which infuriated her but no matter how she scolded, he took no notice, but kept scuttling behind the sink and the big kitchen table, scouring out the preserving pans, and arranging the jars on trays, ready for filling.

The last straw came when he dropped a whole tray load on his way to the pantry. Hot jam splattered everywhere. A blob landed on his foot and he leaped around the kitchen roaring with pain, bumping into the dresser, sending plates and cups flying and upsetting a basket of clean laundry into the jammy mess.

Rosie, beside herself with fury, chased him out into the yard, telling him never to come back. But the next morning, as she lay in bed, telling herself to get up and get started and not wanting to, for it was a chilly day and the bed was warm, she heard the comforting scrape of the shovel and the slam of the oven door. He was back in spite of her!

Things went on in this fashion for some time. The Grogoch worked hard, but he was in the way more and more and no matter how many times she told him to go, he always reappeared he next morning.

Rosie was at her wits end. None of her neighbours had any idea what tot do until one suggested consulting a Fairy Doctor, who lived some twenty miles away. Rosie began saving up the money for the bus fare, but it all got spent, because it was their turn for the Stations.

In those days, The Stations occurred every few years. The parish priest would come and celebrate a Mass in one of the houses in the area. All those in the locality attended and church dues were collected.

Although there was a certain amount of pride attached to being chosen, it also involved a huge amount of work and expense, since the yard had to be brushed and tidied, the outbuildings white-washed, and the house painted inside and out. Everything that could be washed was washed and what could not, was scrubbed, mats were beaten, windows cleaned and food prepared.

There always had to be at least one bottle of whiskey, so that the priest could have 'a drop' when he came into the parlour for his breakfast, and the rest of the men were supplied with porter. Sometimes a bottle of port was laid in for the ladies or perhaps some sweet sherry on which they got quite giggly round the kitchen fire. In big farms they often had a whole barrel of porter and several bottles of 'the hard stuff' but the McCabes just did what they could.

The neighbours brought in food to augment the usual cold chicken and ham and a special meal was served in the parlour for the priest and various chosen men, usually the 'warm' farmers of the area. It was conducted almost in silence, the participants mostly too shy to volunteer a remark and the priest making great efforts to draw them out, while they all listened enviously to the babble of conversation from the kitchen and, as time progressed, the occasional slightly raucous song from the back kitchen where the porter reposed in a crate under the table.

The Grogoch had been his usual helpful self and Rosie had been glad of his assistance with some of the heavier jobs, but he got in her way enough to drive her to distraction so she sent him out to help her husband in the yard, which possibly explained why overnight the house was painted a flaming salmon pink instead of the cream she wanted. However, she said nothing for she knew he would not listen and anyway she did want his help with the large amount of washing up these occasions always brought with them.

Secretly she was looking forward to saying airily, 'Oh, leave it, the Grogoch will do it.'

And so she did, with a smile and a cock of her pretty head. Alas for Rosie! Nobody told her that the Little People never stay in a house where a priest has been and the morning after the event she came down to a cold kitchen and a mountain of dirty china and cutlery!

Fairy Animals

Fairy animals are usually horses or dogs, and always black, with red eyes. They are not often seen nowadays, but in long ago times, the horses used to appear without warning on lonely roads, grazing 'the long meadow' as the roadside grass was often called. Most people rode or drove horses in those days, so they were a great temptation to the footsore traveller. The horses appeared docile and would walk beside him nudging his pocket for a bit of bread. If he succumbed and got on the creature's back, it was transformed in an instant, taking off at a gallop, flying over hedges and ditches in its path with its unwilling passenger hanging on for dear life, afraid to throw himself off in case of injury. Where they ended up is a mystery for only one of them ever returned having been brave enough to throw himself off as they crossed a bog.

There was also, in the West, a strange black hen, which used to appear from nowhere and take up residence in someone's farmyard. Now folk who keep chickens (not the unfortunate battery fowl, which are a fright to God and should not be allowed) know that a black hen is not only the tastiest to eat but also the cleverest.

The black hen was the prettiest, daintiest bird, with shining blue-black feathers and bold orange eyes. She pecked around the stackyard with the other hens and pulled worms our of the manure heap with the best of them. If she was well treated, and the farm animals were flourishing, she would stay for a while, then disappear. Although they searched for her, she was not seen again, but the farmer and his wife would awake one morning to find a gift of something they had longed to get, but could not afford, on their doorstep.

If, on the other hand, the farmer was lazy and careless, the gift would be a huge pile of best quality manure, so large he could not open the door and had to get out of the window. It would take days for him to spread it on his land, and by the end of that he was no longer lazy. The gifts were always useful in some way, although that farmer might not have appreciated his present.

Some say the little black hen was the queen of that part of the country, and chose this disguise to find out if her subjects were peaceful and happy.

Fairy dogs get much pleasure from chasing their victims. They lie in wait in ditches, often frequenting a certain stretch of lonely road; large black creatures about the size of wolfhounds, their red eyes shining in the dark. In the days of horse and even bicycle transport, many a rider returning home at night heard a scurrying upon the road behind him, and looked back to see the red eyes and drooling mouth of a fairy dog. Fortunately these beasts do not seem to catch their victims. Their pleasure appears to lie in seeing someone riding for dear life. History does not relate how many people died from exhaustion on reaching safety.

One unfortunate cyclist saw the glow beside the road one night as he returned from work and thinking that someone had fallen into the dyke, cycle and all, got off his machine to offer assistance, only to find himself face to face with a fairy dog. You may be sure he remounted at speed and pedalled off fast as he could, but the beast padded easily after him despite all his efforts, and it was not until the lights of his neighbour's cow byre shone out across the road that the creature left him.

An enterprising night angler, walking home after a rewarding session poaching at the tail of a salmon pool belonging to Lord Muskerry, suddenly found that he was accompanied by a large black dog with an inordinate interest in his fishing creel. Indeed the creature was butting it with his nose.

''Gwan out o' that!' he shouted furiously.

The dog continued its sniffing. Suddenly, it raised its head and growled. The fisherman, frozen with

fright, gazed into two angry red eyes, unable to move a muscle. The beast snarled—

Suddenly his legs began to work and he was running along the road as fast as he could. Yet still the dog followed, loping easily behind him. Realizing that he could not outrun it, he dipped swiftly into his creel and flung the first fish he could find, a fine five pound salmon, at it. There was the sound of crunching and he looked back, just once, to see it crouched on the road, enjoying its meal.

Lord Muskerry's fish were left in peace after that episode.

Indeed, fairy dogs were still sometimes seen in the country, mostly in winter, when the dark sets in early, up until the mid-1940s. A labourer, cycling home on a quiet road every night, reported the presence of a large black dog which jumped out of the ditch at the same place each time he passed. It made no effort to chase him but ran beside the bike, obviously enjoying itself, until he reached his house, then melted away, but he was able to note the red eyes. Was this the last of the fairy creatures?

Some animals look quite normal, but have fairy powers. There is the tale of Seaneen. He was a fine, handsome young man, but alas he did not have a lot of money. He was walking to the fair in a nearby town one bright summer morning. The birds sang, the sun shone and the air was scented with the meadowsweet and honeysuckle growing along the roadside. Seaneen was feeling happy for he had five bright shillings to spend at the fair and whiled away the journey trying to decide what he would buy with them.

On the outskirts of a small village, he came upon some young lads tormenting a little mouse they had caught.

'Wouldn't you leave the poor little creature alone!' exclaimed Seaneen. 'Come here to me an' I'll give you sixpence for to buy Peggy's Leg.'

The boys were delighted—'Peggy's Leg', as your Irish grandmother would know, was similar to the bright pink sticks of 'rock' that used to be sold at British seaside resorts, only Peggy's Leg was usually thinner, pale fawn in colour, tasted of butter and brown sugar and was not nearly so sticky! Off ran the children, and Seaneen picked up the little mouse. Its tiny heart was beating fast and its bright little eyes were bulging with fright. Not knowing what to do, he slipped it into his pocket and continued on his way.

Presently he caught up with some bigger boys who had something in a cloth bag, which they were beating with sticks.

'What have you there, lads?' asked Seaneen.

'Don't know—some class of rat,' said the biggest boy, opening the bag for Seaneen to look.

'Ah, no. 'Tis a weasel!' exclaimed Seaneen. 'Do ye not know they do keep the rabbits down, so they don't be eating the crops? Ye shouldn't be beating that fella at all! What'd your Da say if he caught ye at it? Will ye let me have him an' I'll give ye somethin' better.'

The boys were quite content to sell the little animal to him for a shilling and, putting it in the straw creel he carried, Seaneen went on. He had not gone far when he came across a couple with a horse and cart. Tied to the back of it was an elderly donkey. They explained that it was too old to work and they were taking it to the knacker to be slaughtered. Seaneen had a tender heart.

'Will ye sell him to me?' he asked.

They were glad to, though it cost him nearly all the money he had left. Seaneen was pleased with this purchase, hopped on the donkey's back and set off along the road. They stopped to eat their lunch under the hedge in a field by the river. Seaneen shared his bread and cheese with the mouse and the weasel, while the donkey enjoyed some grass. The river flowed gently past them, rippling and murmuring in the sunlight and Seaneen fell asleep for a while. He was woken suddenly by a huge man who came running into the field, shouting at him for daring to enter it.

In vain Seaneen tried to explain that he did not know the field belonged to the giant; there was no notice forbidding trespassers—he was very sorry—but the huge man would not listen. He yelled for his servants and with their help pushed Seaneen into a big wooden chest, which he tied up and flung into the river. The animals were most upset.

'We must try to rescue him,' squeaked the mouse.

'He was good to us,' agreed the weasel.

'Come, get on my back and we'll go down the river,' said the donkey.

They set off downstream and presently saw the chest which had stuck against a small island in midstream. The donkey swam across with the mouse clinging to his ear and the weasel hanging onto his mane. When they reached the chest, the mouse and the weasel nibbled and gnawed at the cords until Seaneen was able to get out. He was delighted to see them and they sat down by the water to get their breath back after the excitement.

Looking into the river, Seaneen caught sight of a strange, many-coloured, egg-shaped stone, but it was too deep for him to fish it out. The weasel swam down, picked it up in his mouth and brought it to land. They all admired the beautiful swirling colours.

'Thank you, weasel,' said Seaneen. 'You have all been so good to me! I wish I had a fine house and garden where we could all live together and enjoy ourselves!'

The words were hardly out of his mouth when they found themselves in front of a fine stone-built house, standing in a neat garden shaded by trees. The door was open and inside it was furnished with everything anyone would ever need. They were not long in taking up residence, I can tell you and later on Seaneen met Mary Malone, and carried her over the threshold on their wedding day. After that, they all lived happily together to the end of their lives.

Sometimes the Little People will take the form of animals themselves. There is a story from the Northwest about one such.

In the coastal regions, in order to save the fields near the farmhouse for the winter, the women used to drive the cows up into the hills to graze on patches of good grass among the heather and bracken in summer. Their menfolk would come up to build little shelters for them among the boulders on the hillside; they made themselves beds of heather and had a great time gossiping together and knitting stockings and jerseys for the winter, waiting until it was time for milking.

One day, one woman happened to remark that she did not seem to be getting as much milk from her cow as she usually did and the others agreed. The next day, as they sat waiting on the hillside, a hare started to run among the cattle. She sat up on her hind legs and sucked at their udders and the cows stood quietly as if they were in their stalls at home. The women shouted, the cows kicked up their heels and the hare ran away.

When the men came to fetch the big buckets of milk which would be turned into butter, the women told them about the cheeky hare. They came early the next day and saw that the women had not been codding. There was the hare, sucking away at the cows, for all the world as if she owned them. They ran after her and pelted her with stones but she doubled back and escaped them.

The next day they came up with Thady Tobin and his two hounds. These were mighty hunters and had never been known to fail in capturing their prey. When the hare came, he set on the dogs but she led them a mighty dance in and out of the gorse bushes and across the rocky hillside, leaving the cattle far behind. At last she began to tire and Thady, being a merciful man and having enjoyed his day's hunting, called off his hounds and went home.

Some months later, that same Thady lost a horse he was particularly fond of and scoured the place for it. During the search, he came across a little stone cottage thatched with grass nestling in a secluded valley among the hills. He was thirsty and went to ask for a sup of water. A little old lady in a green skirt came out.

'Ah! 'Tis yourself, Thady Tobin,' she said. 'Sit ye down on the old chair by the door an' I'll bring ye a mug o' milk.'

'How come ye know me an' I don't know you?' asked Thady.

'Did ye never hear the saying, "There's more knows Tom Fool than Tom Fool knows"?' cackled the little woman. 'Ye were good to me once an' called off the dogs. Now, one kind deed deserves another. Sit ye there an' I'll fetch your pony while you do be drinkin' the milk.'

So saying, she suddenly turned into a hare, and before Thady had finished his mug, she was back with the horse.

Thady was delighted. He thanked her heartily, got on the horse and took himself home. Ever after that, Thady gave up hunting hares. Who knows? The next hare he chased might not have been so forgiving.

How to Manage the Gentry

As you will have noticed, the Gentry never stay in a house where there is a member of the clergy and they will not enter a church. Sometimes, if they were particularly troublesome, the priest would come and bless the house and the farmyard, reading from his breviary and sprinkling holy water everywhere. The Little People avoid such things like the plague.

Salt sprinkled on doorsteps and windowsills will also keep them out of the house, but if they are not troublesome, the gift of a saucer of creamy milk, left out at night, will please them and you may find your hens laying exceptionally well and your cows letting down their milk with ease.

Good People everywhere are afraid of iron, in fact of any metal other than silver, gold or copper. In long ago days, mothers would sometimes stitch tiny bright bells on a child's dress as protection, just as brasses hanging from the harness kept their plough horses safe.

Sometimes in farmyards you will see the old iron hoop from a barrel, or a plough chain hanging on the wall outside the cowshed and a worn horseshoe nailed above the half-door of the stable, or above the kitchen door. These must always be with the open end upwards, otherwise the luck will run out. If they are found by chance in the fields or on the roadway, they are thought to be exceptionally lucky.

A daisy chain will protect you in the fields. Indeed, children playing outside during the summer were encouraged by their mothers to make and wear them, often with the bribe of a toffee or liquorice 'bootlace' for the best one. A twig of broom or sprig of St John's Wort is also used to keep the Gentry at bay and

A sock under the bed, a knife under the pillow,
Churchyard mould or Cross of willow.

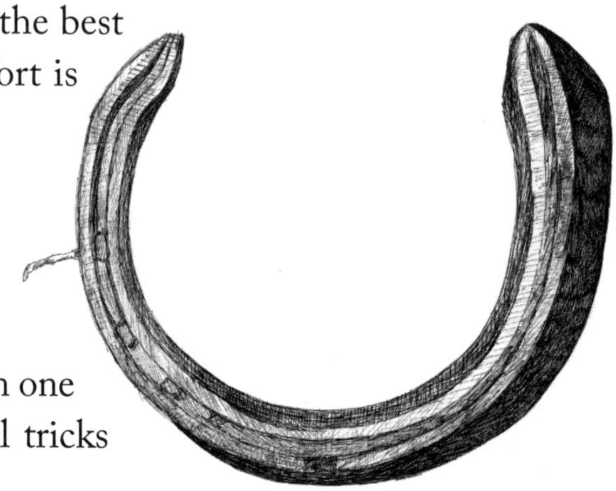

Best of all, if you are lucky enough to find one, is a four-leaved shamrock. There was once a showman whose mother was said to have been one of the Sidhe. Certainly he could do wonderful tricks

and made his living going from one fair to another in the province of Munster. He would make coloured sparks jump from his fingers and dance a jig in the air. He had a reed pipe with which he could call a flock of birds to perch on his arms and head and a little mat which he rolled up and shook out to send toffees and sweets flying among the crowd. However his most popular act involved a little brightly coloured cock, which travelled everywhere in a bag on his back. He would harness the cock with twine to a great log of wood, which the bird would then pull around the circle of spectators. Everyone applauded and those who had seen it done never tired of telling their neighbours, until the neighbours were mad to see it themselves and followed him about begging him to let them see the little cock that was 'strong as a horse'.

One day, as he was performing on the outskirts of a village to the delight of a small crowd, a man passed by carrying an armful of green grass for a cow that was sick.

'What in the wide, earthly world are ye all up to?' he asked.

'Sure, don't ye see the cockeen an' he pullin' the big log o' wood?' said an onlooker.

The man peered over the spectators' heads with interest.

'Sure, aren't ye all a fine pack av fine eejits,' he said scornfully, ''tis only an old piece of straw he does be draggin' after him!'

'Moryiah (nonsense)!' they cried, ''Tis you eyes are bad—maybe you should get glasses!'

The man was about to protest but the showman drew him aside and offered to buy the bundle of grass. Sensing the opportunity for a bargain, the fellow at last sold it to him for a very inflated price and walked off happily jingling the coins in his pocket. But he turned back, for he could not resist one more look at the little cock to massage his ego a little further. You can imagine his shock when he saw, yes, a little brightly coloured gamecock, strolling round the circle, dragging a huge log after him.

Meanwhile, the showman had given the grass to his young son who travelled with him.

'Throw it in the stream, boyeen, and leave it go down with the water,' he instructed.

Later that night, when they pitched their old tent up on the moors, the boy asked why his father had thrown away the grass.

'There was a four-leaved shamrock among it, boy. That's why the fella saw through the trick. Couldn't have that, now could we?' said his father.

Sometimes one forgets the old ways and the Little People are quick to take advantage. After his mother died, Eddie Casey lived alone on his little farm. He kept it very well. The walls were lime-washed, the thatch renewed every few years and his potatoes and cabbages carefully tended. His few animals thrived and at milking time he always left a saucer of milk on the cowshed windowsill for the Good People, just as his mother had taught him when he was a boy. One night, however, he had a young cow calving and he forgot to do so. He was sitting on a truss of straw in the byre, the old oil lantern, called by country people a 'hurricane butty', at his feet, when a wind suddenly got up. There was a sudden crash as a bucket on the coping around the well blew off and went rolling across the yard.

When he looked out, the air was thick with dust and straws, whirling round like a sheegwee and seemed to be full of tiny voices shouting at him. He took another bucket and drew up some water to fill the kettle for a cup of tea. He had nearly reached his door when an extra strong gust swept the bucket from his hand. The water was spilled and he had to go back for more, while shrieks of wild laughter rang in his ears.

He was very tired and this happened three times before he realized that it was a fairy wind. Stamping into the kitchen in a fury, and suddenly remembering what his mother had told him, he took off his coat and put it on again inside out. This time he reached the well and carried back his bucket without interference, although the air around him throbbed with little moaning cries.

'Sorry I am I ever crossed ye,' he shouted as he fetched a saucer of milk to set on the windowsill. 'An' would you ever leave off tormentin' me. I've the cow to see to an' me heart is broke for the want of a cup o' tea!'

The wind died and after he had finished his tea, he went back to the byre and there was the prettiest little white heifer calf you did ever see. What did he name her? Sheegwee, of course.

Another way to avert trouble is to use this blessing. 'Today is Monday, may God be between us and all harm.' The day of the week must always be mentioned and woe betide you if you get it wrong!

One last thing. During your rambles in the countryside, always carry a piece of iron or steel; an old nail will do, and a crust of bread in your pocket to keep the Good People away. The crust is in case you step on Hungry Grass.

Hungry Grass? It is another trick of the Little People. Sometimes they bewitch a piece of grass, so that the unfortunates who tread on it are seized with a ravenous hunger, becoming so weak that they fall to the ground and cannot summon enough strength to continue on their way. A bite of bread will break the spell and foil those who are doubtless waiting about in the vicinity to get a good laugh at the success of their plan.

It has been said that Hungry Grass is not a charm of the Good Folk at all, but emanations given forth from where a famine grave was located. So many died in the Great Potato Famine that there was not always room enough to bury them in the churchyard and graves were dug wherever there was space, not always in the vicinity of a church. The grass which grew over the mounds above them was said to hold forever the trace of their suffering. Indeed, even today it is considered very bad manners to walk over any grave.

Enjoy your rambling. Yes, I know you do not believe the half of it; you have cars and houses full of grand appliances, sure you never used a washboard in your life or scrubbed the kitchen floor on your hands and knees, or lifted your head from digging the garden to hear a hammer tapping behind the hedge. A thrush or a blackbird eating a snail you'd say it was and maybe you'd be right—or maybe not.

There's still room in the beautiful country for You Know Who to exist alongside of ourselves and who's to say they don't. Sheegwees still dance across farmyards. And, maybe, if the fella that's up on the new tractor, ploughing the home field twice as fast as the old horse, was to look in his lunch bag under the hedge, he might find his bottle of milk empty and the top still on it. How did *that* happen? He hasn't been married long, not long enough for his wife to be *that* careless. In fact, if you listen carefully, you might even hear the wild laughter all round after you've stepped into a boghole on a perfectly innocent path—Over here, you never can tell with Them—

The Little People of Ireland

Aine Connor

Illustrations by Hammond Journeaux

SOMERVILLE PRESS

Somerville Press
Dromore, Bantry
Co. Cork, Ireland

ISBN 978 0 9545724 57

Printed in Spain.